First Facts

Spiders
Trapdoor Spiders

by Molly Kolpin

Consultant:
Pedro Barbosa, PhD
Department of Entomology
University of Maryland, College Park

CAPSTONE PRESS
a capstone imprint

First Facts is published by Capstone Press,
151 Good Counsel Drive, P.O. Box 669, Mankato, Minnesota 56002.
www.capstonepub.com

Copyright © 2011 by Capstone Press, a Capstone imprint.
All rights reserved.
No part of this publication may be reproduced in whole or in part, or stored in a retrieval system, or transmitted in any form or by any means, electronic, mechanical, photocopying, recording, or otherwise, without written permission of the publisher. For information regarding permission, write to Capstone Press, 151 Good Counsel Drive, P.O. Box 669, Dept. R, Mankato, Minnesota 56002.
Printed in the United States of America in Melrose Park, Illinois.
032010
005742LKF10

 Books published by Capstone Press are manufactured with paper containing at least 10 percent post-consumer waste.

Library of Congress Cataloging-in-Publication Data
Kolpin, Molly.
 Trapdoor spiders / by Molly Kolpin.
   p. cm.—(First facts. Spiders)
 Includes bibliographical references and index.
 Summary: "A brief introduction to trapdoor spiders, including their habitat, food, and life cycle"—Provided by publisher.
 ISBN 978-1-4296-4521-8 (library binding)
 1. Trap-door spiders—Juvenile literature. I. Title. II. Series.
QL458.4.K65 2011
595.4′4—dc22   2010002257

Editorial Credits
Lori Shores, editor; Veronica Correia, designer; Eric Manske, production specialist

Photo Credits
Alamy/blickwinkel, cover
Getty Images Inc./Photolibrary/David Fox, 13
Nature Picture Library/Hans Christoph Kappel, 1, 11; Ingo Arndt, 21
© Peter J. Bryant/Biological Photo Service, 19
Photo Researchers Inc/Dr. Paul A. Zahl, 8, 20; James H. Robinson, 16;
    Nature's Images, 7
Photoshot/Bruce Coleman, 5, 15

Essential content terms are **bold** and are defined at the bottom of the page where they first appear.

Table of Contents

Shy Spiders 4
Plump Bodies 6
Building a Home 9
Knock, Knock 10
Finding Trapdoor Spiders 12
Hungry Hunters 14
Dinnertime 17
Tiny Spiders 18
Super Silk 20

Amazing but True! 21
Glossary 22
Read More 23
Internet Sites 23
Index 24

Shy Spiders

Trapdoor spiders spend most of their lives underground. Even above ground, people don't see trapdoor spiders very often. Their dark bodies blend in with the dirt around them.

Spider Fact!

Trapdoor spiders' legs look shiny as if they've been polished.

Plump Bodies

Trapdoor spiders are related to tarantulas. But these **arachnids** are smaller and have less hair. Most trapdoor spiders are only 1 inch (2.5 centimeters) long. Like other spiders, they have two main body parts and eight legs.

Spider Fact!

The hair on trapdoor spiders' bodies helps them learn about their surroundings.

arachnid—an animal with four pairs of legs and no backbone, wings, or antennae

Building a Home

Trapdoor spiders build and live in **burrows**. They line their burrows with a mixture of dirt and spit. Then they cover the walls with **silk**.

Spider Fact!

Trapdoor spiders sometimes build walls around their burrows to keep water out.

burrow—a tunnel or hole in the ground where an animal lives
silk—a string made by spiders

Knock, Knock

A trapdoor spider makes a door from silk and dirt. One side of the door attaches to the burrow with silk. When **predators** try to get in, the spider holds the door shut.

Spider Fact!

Some trapdoor spiders dig extra tunnels in their burrows. If an enemy gets in, the spider runs out a back door.

predator—an animal that hunts other animals for food

Finding Trapdoor Spiders

Trapdoor spiders live in warm places. Many live in Australia and Asia. In the United States, most trapdoor spiders live in the South.

where trapdoor spiders live

Most trapdoor spiders build burrows in dry, loose dirt. Some trapdoor spiders build burrows near rivers to catch little fish.

Hungry Hunters

Trapdoor spiders hunt at night. The spider pokes its front legs out of its burrow and waits for **prey**. The hairs on the spider's legs feel when an insect comes close. Then the spider dashes out and bites the insect.

Spider Fact!

Trapdoor spiders can rush out and catch prey in less than half a second!

prey—an animal hunted by another animal for food

leg hair

Dinnertime

Trapdoor spiders squirt juices from their **fangs** into their prey's body. The juices turn the body into a soupy liquid. Then the trapdoor spider sucks up the prey.

Spider Fact!

Trapdoor spiders usually eat small insects. Large trapdoor spiders also eat small lizards.

fang—a long, pointed toothlike mouthpart

Tiny Spiders

Male and female trapdoor spiders mate in the summer. Then the female spider lays hundreds of eggs. She places them in an **egg sac** on the burrow wall.

A few weeks later, **spiderlings** hatch from the eggs. They stay with their mother for up to eight months. Spiderlings leave when they can dig their own burrows.

egg sac—a small pouch made of silk that holds spider eggs
spiderling—a young spider

Life Cycle of a Trapdoor Spider

Newborn
Spiderlings look like adults, only smaller.

eggs

Young
Trapdoor spiders make their burrows wider as they grow bigger.

Adult
Male trapdoor spiders live for about one year. Females can live up to 20 years.

Super Silk

Trapdoor spiders use silk to make trip wires. When an insect stumbles on the silk string, the spider leaps out. The silk also lets the spider know when danger is near.

Amazing but True!

silk bag

Some trapdoor spiders hang silk bags of leftover bug parts by their doors. If an enemy gets in, the spider pulls on the silk. The bug parts fall out and block the enemy's way.

Glossary

arachnid (uh-RACK-nid)—an animal with four pairs of legs and no backbone, wings, or antennae

burrow (BUHR-oh)—a tunnel or hole in the ground where an animal lives

egg sac (EG SAK)—a small pouch made of silk that holds spider eggs

fang (FANG)—a long, pointed toothlike mouthpart

mate (MATE)—to join together to produce young

predator (PRED-uh-tur)—an animal that hunts other animals for food

prey (PRAY)—an animal hunted by another animal for food

silk (SILK)—a string made by spiders

spiderling (SPYE-dur-ling)—a young spider

Read More

Bishop, Nic. *Spiders.* New York: Scholastic Nonfiction, 2007.

Goldish, Meish. *Tricky Trapdoor Spiders.* No Backbone! New York: Bearport Publishing, 2009.

Trueit, Trudi Strain. *Spiders.* Creepy Critters. New York: Marshall Cavendish Benchmark, 2009.

Internet Sites

FactHound offers a safe, fun way to find Internet sites related to this book. All of the sites on FactHound have been researched by our staff.

Here's all you do:

Visit *www.facthound.com*

FactHound will fetch the best sites for you!

Index

arachnids, 6

biting, 14
bodies, 4, 6
burrows, 9, 13, 14, 18, 19
    building, 9
    doors, 10, 21

eating, 17
eggs, 18
egg sacs, 18

fangs, 17

habitat, 4, 12–13
hair, 6, 14
hunting, 14

legs, 6, 14
life cycle, 18, 19
life span, 19

predators, 10, 20, 21
prey, 13, 14, 17, 20

range, 12

silk, 9, 10, 20, 21
size, 6, 19
spiderlings, 18, 19

tarantulas, 6
trip wires, 20

SAYVILLE LIBRARY
88 GREENE AVENUE
SAYVILLE, NY 11782

MAR 0 4 2011